The Musicians of Bremen

A TALE FROM GERMANY

RETOLD BY
Jane Yolen

ILLUSTRATED BY
John Segal

Simon & Schuster Books for Young Readers

SIMON & SCHUSTER BOOKS FOR YOUNG READERS

An imprint of Simon & Schuster Children's Publishing Division

1230 Avenue of the Americas, New York, New York 10020

SIMON & SCHUSTER BOOKS FOR YOUNG READERS is a trademark of Simon & Schuster.

Book design by Paul Zakris. The text for this book is set in 18-point Venetian.

The illustrations are rendered in watercolor.

Manufactured in the United States of America.

First Edition

10 9 8 7 6 5 4 3 2 1

Library of Congress Cataloging-in-Publication Data

Yolen, Jane.

The musicians of Bremen : a tale from Germany / retold by Jane Yolen ; illustrated by John Segal.

p.   cm.

Summary: Four animals who are no longer wanted by their masters set out to become musicians
in the town of Bremen, but along the way they encounter a den of thieves.

ISBN 0-689-80501-2

1. Fairy tales. 2. Folklore—Germany. I. Segal, John, ill. II. Title.

PZ8.Y78Mu   1996   398.2'0943045—dc20   [E]   94-30732

For Maddison Jane Piatt,
happy first birthday, March 25
—J. Y.

To Joshua, with love
—J. S.

There was once an old donkey whose better days were past. One day he overheard his master tell the butcher, "Best come for him tomorrow." So without waiting for the next day to dawn, Donkey ran away toward Bremen. "Perhaps I can become a musician there," he thought. "I am loud enough. That will be the life!"

As he went along, he saw an odd lump in the road. When he got closer, he saw it was no lump at all but an old dog.

"Hello, Growler," said Donkey. "Why do you lie so still? I thought you were a lump in the road."

"A lump I would have been had I stayed at home," said Dog. "My master wished to kill me, for I am too old to run with his pack. So I ran away instead."

"I was treated just the same," said Donkey. "So I am off to Bremen to become a musician and play the kettledrum."

"Can I come, too?" asked Dog. "I am loud enough. I shall play the guitar."

"That will be the life!" said Donkey, and off they went.

A little farther on they saw an odd lump in the road. When they got closer, they saw it was no lump at all but an old cat.

"Hello, Whiskers," said Donkey and Dog. "Why do you lie so still? We thought you were a lump in the road."

"And so I should have been had I stayed home," said Cat. "My mistress wished to kill me, for I am too old to catch mice. So I ran away instead."

Donkey and Dog nodded. "We were treated just the same."

"I am going to Bremen to play the kettledrum," said Donkey.

"And I to play guitar," added Dog.

"Can I come, too?" asked Cat. "I am loud enough. I could sing."

"That will be the life!" Donkey and Dog replied, and they all went off together.

A little farther on, they saw an odd lump in the road. When they got closer, they saw it was no lump at all but an old rooster.

"Hello, Red-Comb," said the three. "Why do you sit so still? We thought you were a lump in the road."

"And so I should have been if I had stayed at home," said Rooster. "Cook wanted to kill me for Sunday dinner, as I am too old to crow every dawn."

Donkey and Dog and Cat all nodded. "We were treated just the same."

"We are running off to Bremen to become musicians," said Cat. "Donkey will play the kettledrum, Dog the guitar, and I will sing."

"Can I come, too?" asked Rooster. "I am loud enough. I can sing bass."

"That will be the life!" they replied, and all four headed on down the road.

But well before they reached Bremen, they came to a wood. Day had turned to night and the forest was filled with shadows. As none of them had eaten since dawn, they were ready to give in to despair. But Rooster flew onto a tree branch and spied a light ahead.

"A light means a house," Cat told them. "Let us go and sing for our supper."

The house was large and commodious. A
fine brass knocker hung on the door. But when
Donkey—who was the tallest—peeked in the
window, to his horror he saw the house was a
robbers' den. Around a great table were a dozen
of the nastiest-looking villains he had ever seen,
counting gold coins into an iron pot. Every
once in a while they would hit one another over
the head with sticks, just for fun.

"As long as robbers are within," he said to
his friends, "we must be without."

Donkey and Rooster thought hard. Dog thought harder. But Cat thought hardest of all, and she came up with a plan.

Donkey put his forefeet on the window.

Dog jumped on Donkey's back.

Cat leaped on Dog's neck.

And last of all Rooster perched on Cat's head. When he landed, he began to crow, louder than at any dawn. Cat began to sing. Dog began to howl. Donkey began to bray. The music was indeed quite loud. And very, very horrible.

The robbers jumped up in great alarm and,

fearing a demon, ran out of the house.

When the robbers were well into the woods, Donkey, Dog, Cat, and Rooster went inside. There they found food and drink, which they swallowed till their stomachs could hold no more. Then they settled themselves down for a nap. Donkey lay on some straw by the front door. Dog lay on a blanket by the back. Cat curled up next to the warm hearth fire, and Rooster flew up to a rafter. Tired from their long journey, and their big meal, and their loud music making, the friends were soon asleep.

But the robbers were not. They huddled cold and frightened until the last of the hearth coals had winked out and the house was quiet and dark. Then the robber chief, who was a bit braver than the rest, said, "Perhaps it was only the wind and not a demon after all. We need to check it out. You, Jock!" He pointed to one robber. "Look about inside and tell us what you find."

Jock did not want to go, but he did as he was told. The house was so quiet and so dark and so still, he went right in. When he saw Cat's glowing eyes (for cats can sleep with their eyes open, you know), he thought they were two coals on the fire.

So he held out a wisp of straw to get a light.
Cat woke with a screech and scratched him.
Dog jumped up and bit him on the leg.

Donkey kicked him in the front. And Rooster, starting up from his perch in the rafters, cried, "COCK-A-DOO, COCK-A-DOO!"

Jock ran back to the woods as fast as he could. "It was no demon," he said to the other robbers, "but much, much worse. There was a witch by the fire who screeched and scratched me. A man by the door stabbed me with a knife. A big policeman by the other door hit me with his billy club. And on a high chair sits a judge, who called me by name saying, 'Jock will do! Jock will do!'"

Well, to a robber, demons are one thing, policeman and judge quite another. They ran off, well past Bremen, and were never heard from again.

As for the four friends, they had enough to eat and to drink, and gold to buy more, so they never needed to move away.

And they never needed to go to Bremen to make music—which would have brought the people of Bremen great relief, had they but known.

NOTE: *This story is known in slightly different versions all through Europe, Asia, and America. This German version from the Brothers Grimm is so well known that in the town of Bremen, brass, wood, and china donkeys, cats, dogs, and roosters are popular items for sale.*